Two children came.

1

They climbed on the furniture.

They jumped on the sofa.

They climbed up the curtains.

They jumped on the bed.

They climbed up the tree.

They jumped on the flowers.

'Oh no!' said Mum.

Biff had an idea.

They climbed up the ladder.

They jumped off the log.

They climbed on the net.

They jumped off the wall.

Everyone was happy.

'What good children!' said Mum.

The children went home.